MY SEARCH FOR A CURE

by J. E. Bright   illustrated by Saxton Moore
based on the screenplay by Zack Penn and Edward Norton

Ready-to-Read

Simon Spotlight
New York   London   Toronto   Sydney

SIMON SPOTLIGHT
An imprint of Simon & Schuster Children's Publishing Division
1230 Avenue of the Americas, New York, New York 10020
The Incredible Hulk, the Movie © 2008 MVL Film Finance LLC. Marvel, The Incredible Hulk, all character name
and their distinctive likenesses: TM & © 2008 Marvel Entertainment, Inc. and its subsidiaries. All Rights Reserve
All rights reserved, including the right of reproduction in whole or in part in any form.
SIMON SPOTLIGHT, READY-TO-READ, and associated colophon are trademarks of Simon & Schuster, Inc.
Manufactured in the United States of America
First Edition 10 9 8 7 6 5 4 3 2 1
ISBN-13: 978-1-4169-6083-6
ISBN-10: 1-4169-6083-X

CHAPTER ONE: Out of Control

My name is Bruce Banner. I used to be a
scientist at a university. My friend
Betty Ross and I worked on a top-secret
project for the United States Army.
We were treating human cells
with gamma rays.

I was so sure of our work that I tested the gamma rays on myself. It was very dangerous, but I thought it was worth the risk.

First Betty injected me with a serum she'd invented to strengthen my cells. Then she zapped me with what should have been a low dose of gamma radiation. But something went wrong, and I got too much radiation.

Suddenly I felt a powerful rage inside.
My cells swelled with mighty energy.
I screamed as my body stretched and
exploded with massive green muscles—
and I became The Hulk. Wild with pain,
I smashed up the lab.

I was so strong and so out of control that I accidentally hurt Betty.

Once the army knew what I had become, they wanted to use me as a weapon. I didn't want to hurt anyone else, so I ran away and went into hiding.

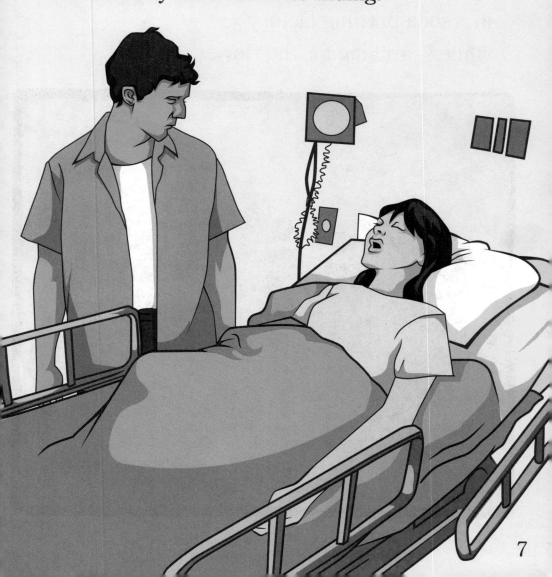

CHAPTER TWO: The Flower

Years later I heard about a scientist with an antidote for gamma radiation. It came from a rare flower that grew in Brazil. So I went to Brazil to look for it. I got an apartment and worked in a soda-bottling factory while searching for the flower.

I avoided people as much as possible, afraid that the army would find me, or someone would make me angry.

To learn how to stay calm, I took martial arts lessons and learned breathing exercises. If I got too upset, I would transform into the wild, muscular monster.

For a few years I had no luck finding the
rare flower. I felt terribly hopeless
and alone. But then the research
scientist who I knew as Mr. Blue
mailed me a book
with information about the flower.

I hired someone from the factory to go into the jungle to get the flower. While I waited, I built a laboratory in my apartment.

Finally the man returned to town—and he had the rare flowers with him!

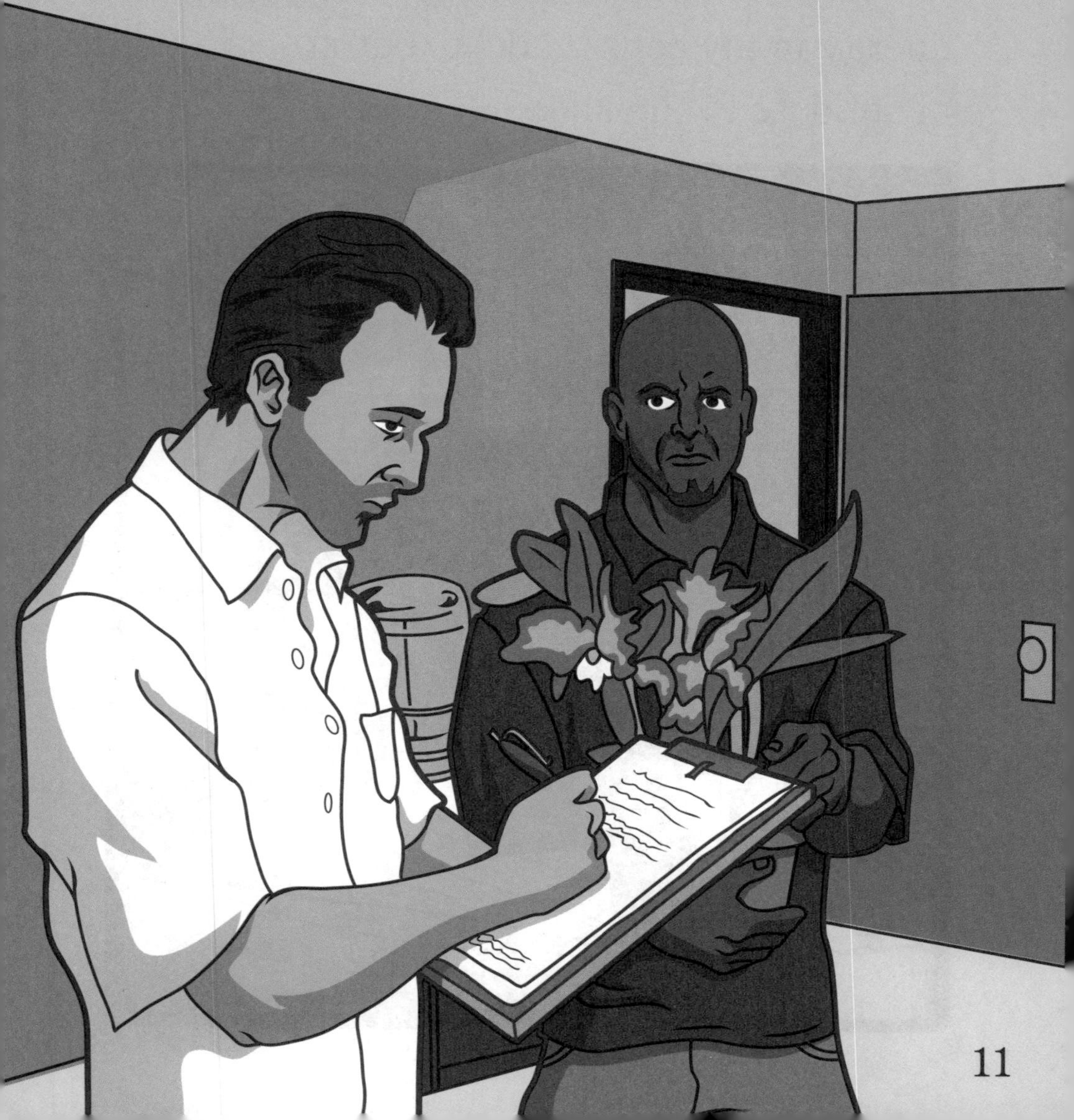

I squeezed the liquid out of the flowers.
Then I spun the liquid in a machine
until the antidote surfaced.

I pricked my finger, and put a drop
of my blood on a glass slide. Under my
microscope I could see the green gamma
energy in my cells. I added a drop
of antidote to the slide.

The purple liquid boiled when it touched the green energy around my cells. For a second I thought it was working!
But then the purple liquid disappeared, and the green stayed in my cells.

Once again my experiment had failed.

I wrote Mr. Blue about my results. He said that my gamma levels must be high, and that I'd need a stronger dose.

I did not have any more of the antidote, but Mr. Blue said he had a large amount in his lab. All he needed was my blood sample.

I stared at the dead flowers. I had no other choice. I made a sample, and I mailed it to Mr. Blue.

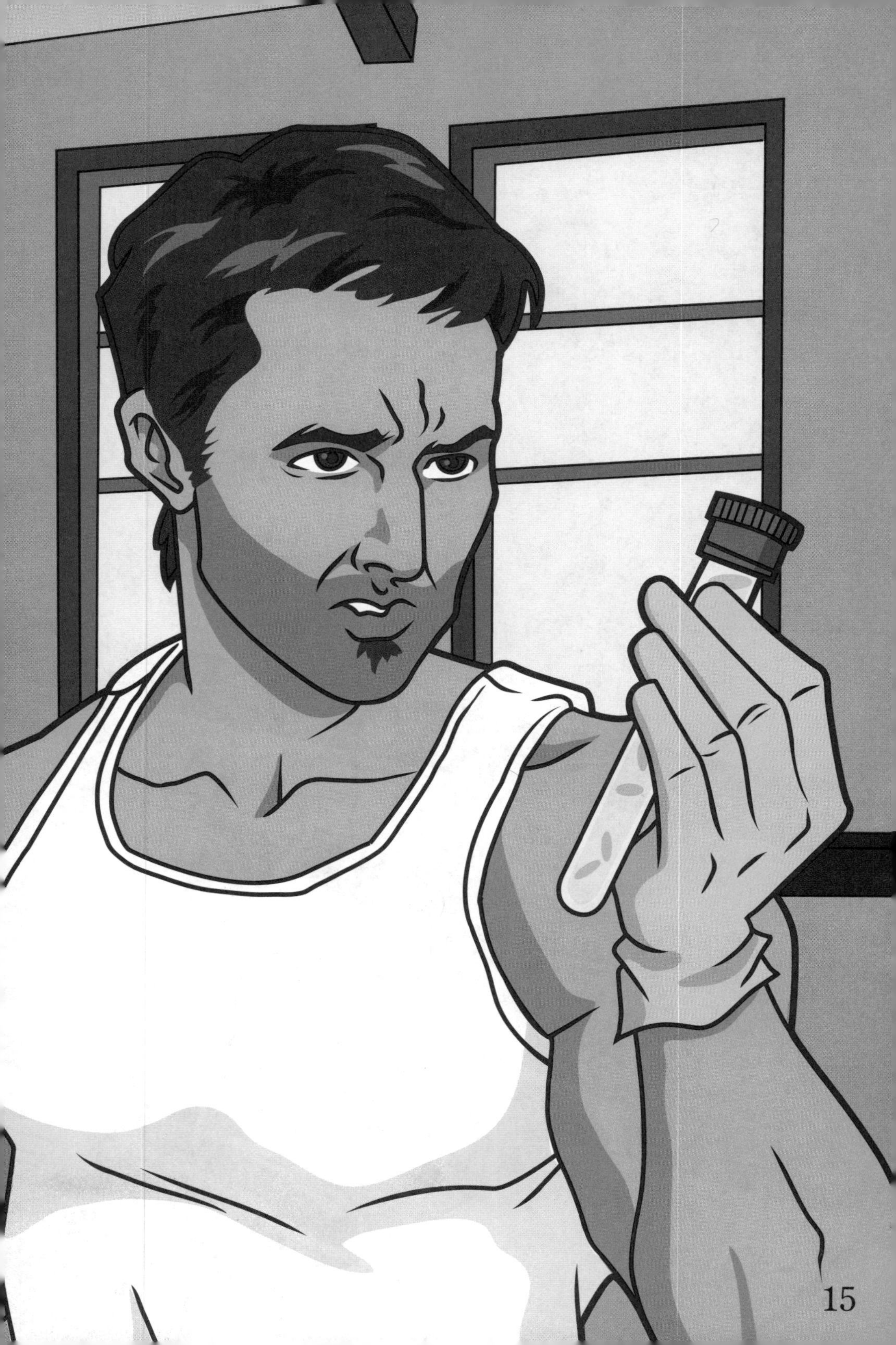

A few days later Mr. Blue wrote that he had created the antidote! I told him that my gamma levels rise when I have episodes.

He said that they could not get higher than when I was first exposed. With the original data from my exposure, he could create the cure!

I knew I needed to get him the data from the experiment at the Maynard lab. It was my only hope.

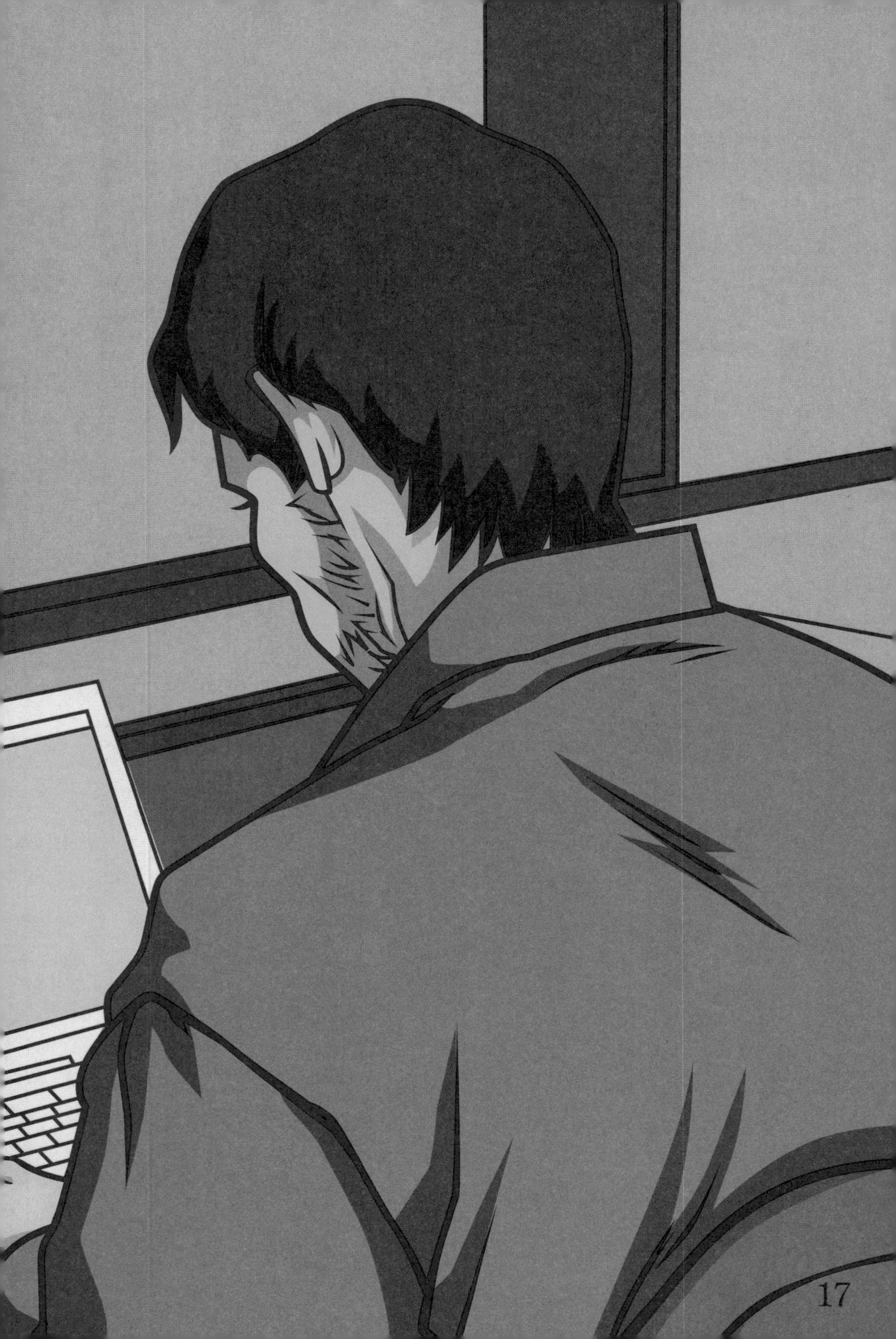

CHAPTER THREE: Blast from the Past

That night the army found me. I was on the run again. But this time I knew exactly where I was running to: Culver Campus.

I returned to the United States,
and went to the university town
where I used to live and work.

My friend Stan owns a pizza place there.
I used a pizza-delivery disguise to get
into the Maynard lab. I finally got
into the database, but all my research
was gone! The army had erased it all.

Once again I felt like I had no hope. That's when Betty saw me. I tried to run away, but Betty talked me into coming to her house.

There she told me that she'd saved all of our research data! She gave me a small data flashcard that held all the information.

Thanks to Betty, I had hope again.

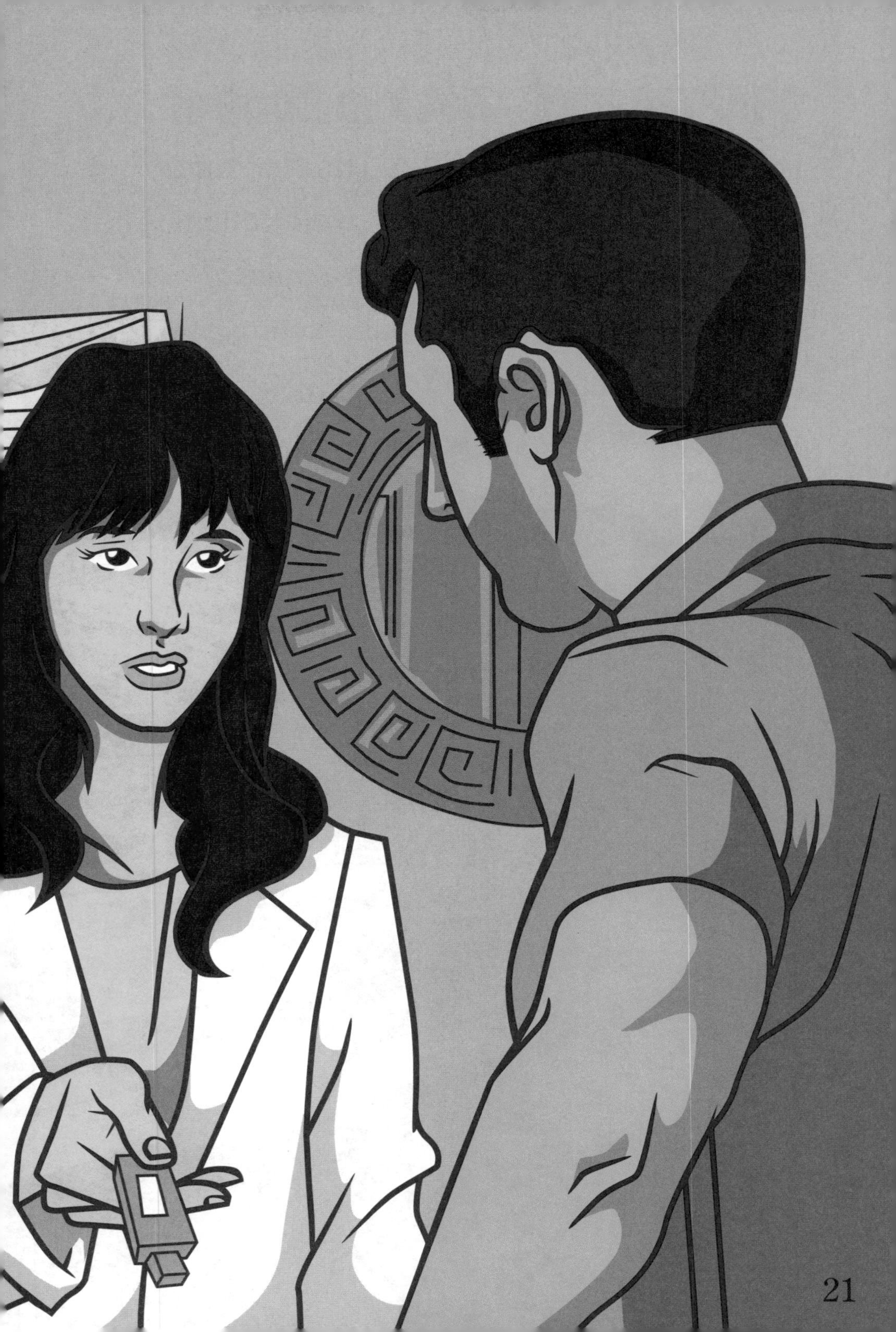

CHAPTER FOUR: Back in Control

Betty also knew Mr. Blue. His real name was Dr. Sterns, and he was well known for his work with the rare Brazilian flower. We e-mailed the data to him, and then went to New York, where he was working.

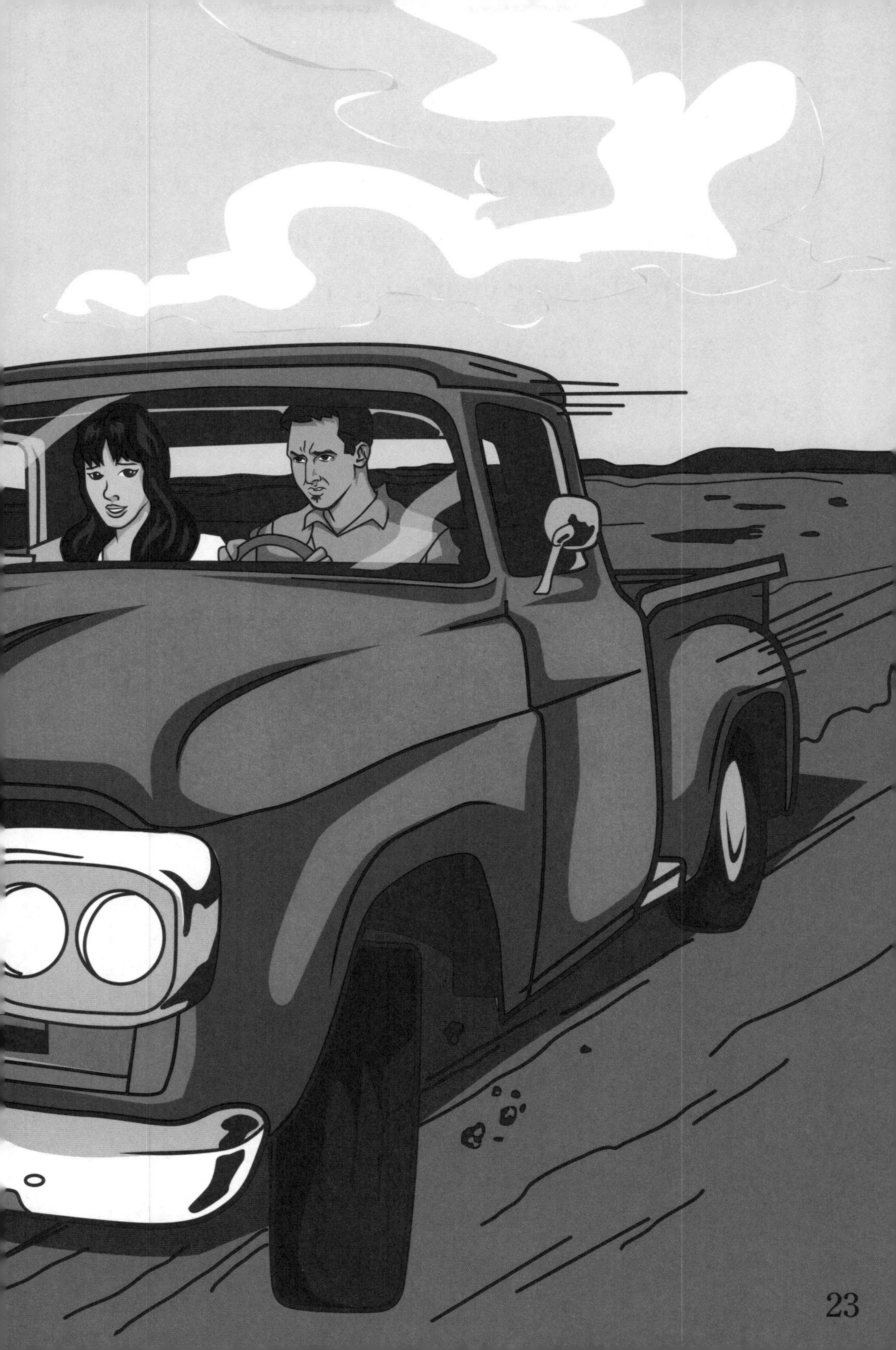

At Empire State University we found Dr. Sterns. He prepared the antidote for me. First I had to turn back into The Hulk, something I never wanted to do again.

"I have to warn you," he said, "if we give you too much antidote, it could be extremely toxic."

"You mean he could die?" asked Betty.

"Well, yes," answered Dr. Sterns.

"If you give me too little," I warned,

"it could be very dangerous for *you*."

"Promise you'll run away if things go bad," I begged Betty.

Then I began to turn into The Hulk. My eyes glowed green, and a green light flashed in my skull. The color washed down my whole body as I changed into a monster made of pure muscle.

"Give him the antidote!" Betty yelled.

Dr. Sterns injected me with the antidote.

Lost in my rage, I fought to escape.
But Betty jumped onto the lab table and
cried, "Stay with me, Bruce!"

The antidote started to work! It wasn't a
complete cure, but now I had some hope!
After I had calmed down, Dr. Sterns told
us he'd duplicated my blood to create
more Hulks.

"Destroy it all now!" I ordered him.
Suddenly, out of the blue, I felt
something stick in my neck.

CHAPTER FIVE: A New Hero

When I awoke, I realized that the
army had found and captured me.
I thought I was caught for good, but
then we heard screaming.
Something was destroying the city.

Dr. Sterns had given a soldier my
blood!

Only The Hulk could stop the
new monster.

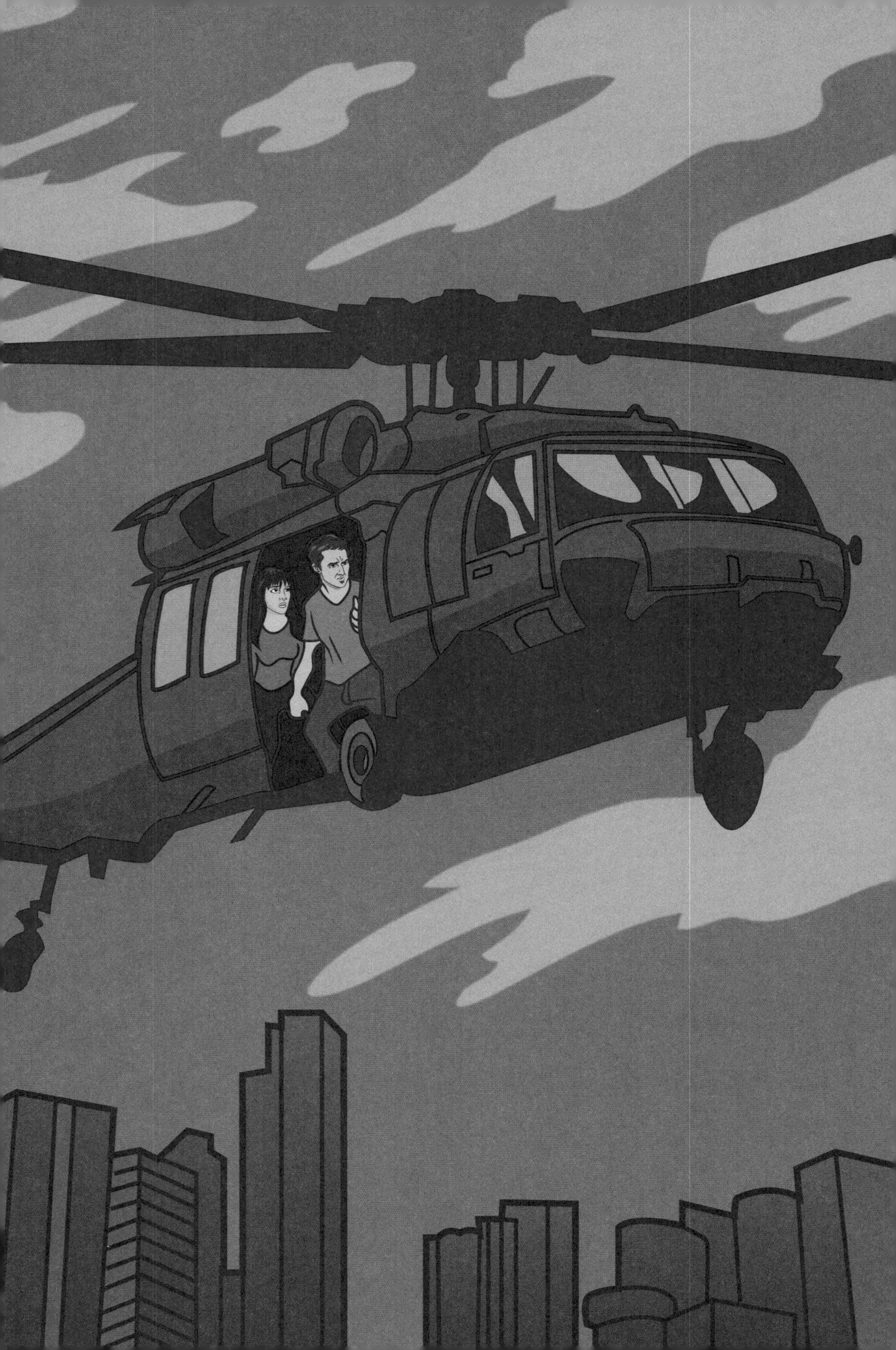

So The Hulk challenged the new monster: The Abomination.

During our fight, somehow, The Hulk realized Betty was in danger! The Abomination held me down, but The Hulk needed to save Betty!

A new strength surged into my muscles.

With the extra power The Hulk saved Betty, and defeated The Abomination.

After that I was on the run again. The army would never leave me alone, so I had to say good-bye to the antidote and Betty.

But I realized that maybe becoming The Hulk is not all bad. Even as The Hulk, I wanted to save Betty.

I still practice my breathing exercises. Now I can also speed up my pulse, and feel power rushing into my body. My eyes flash green, and I start to change. There may never be a permanent cure, but maybe The Hulk is not as bad as I thought.